Cover illustration © 2006 by Ross Collins
Interior illustrations © 2006 by AnnaLaura Cantone,
Ross Collins, Joelle Dreidemy, Andrea Huseinovic
Text © 2006 by Vivian French

First published in the United Kingdom in 2006 by The Chicken House,
2 Palmer Street, Frome, Somerset BA11 1DS.
www.doublecluck.com

Library of Congress Cataloging-in-Publication data available

10 9 8 7 6 5 4 3 2 1   ISBN 0-439-79608-3

06 07 08 09 10

Printed in China
First American edition, June 2006

Designed by Leyah Jensen

The Daddy Goose

TREASURY

as told to VIVIAN FRENCH

Illustrated by AnnaLaura Cantone, Ross Collins,
Joelle Dreidemy, Andrea Huseinovic

The Chicken HOUSE

SCHOLASTIC INC. / NEW YOrk

Meet Daddy Goose!

For hundreds of years little children have heard

About old Mother Goose, a remarkable bird

Whose pockets and baskets are stuffed full of rhyme—

But now is the moment, and now is the time

For a **whoosh!** For a **zoom!** And the **sparkle** of stars

As Daddy Goose circles 'round Venus and Mars,

Then dives with a **vroom!** And a **whizz!** And a **fizz!**

Is he coming to see us? He is! Yes, he is!

He's bringing us stories of "Hey, Diddle, Diddle"

(To tell us just *why* puss was playing a fiddle),

The tale of a clock, and of merry King Cole,

And Little Miss Muffet, with curds in a bowl.

There's Humpty, and Mary, there's Jack and there's Jill.

And where is the black sheep? Why, up on the hill!

For old Mother Goose may have rhymes we know well,

But it's Daddy who knows all the stories to tell!

So pick up this book,
and cuddle up tight,
And let Daddy Goose
tell your story tonight....

CONTENTS

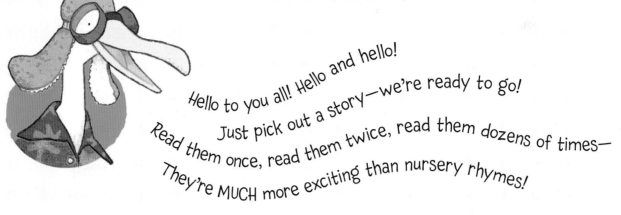

Hello to you all! Hello and hello!
Just pick out a story—we're ready to go!
Read them once, read them twice, read them dozens of times—
They're MUCH more exciting than nursery rhymes!

Hey, Diddle, Diddle

Hey, diddle, diddle,
The cat and the fiddle,
The cow jumped over the moon;
The little dog laughed
To see such fun,
And the dish ran away with the spoon.

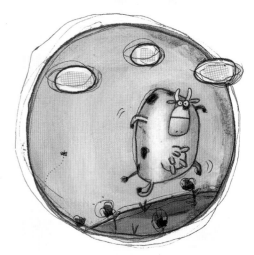

When Lilly the cow was little she didn't like living in a field and eating grass. Not at all. Not one bit. She wanted to hop and skip and run and jump, and be World Famous Indeed. Her mom said, "Don't be silly, Lilly. Cows are never famous." Lilly didn't agree.

One evening, when her mom was napping, Lilly ran away. She hopped and she skipped and she ran, and she jumped right out of the field. Right into town Lilly ran, and there she stopped. The town was very busy. Shopkeepers were shutting up their shops with a clatter. Men and women were hurrying home from work. Children were running home for dinner.

Lilly stood and stared.

"Woof!"

Lilly looked down and saw a little dog. On his arm was a basket, and inside was a grumpy-looking tin dish and an angry-looking silver spoon.

"Hello," said the little dog. "What's your name?"

"Lilly," said Lilly.

The little dog laughed. "My name's Billy," he said. "Billy and Lilly! We'd better stick together."

"All right," said Lilly. "But I've come to town because I want to be a World Famous Cow."

"You don't say?" said Billy. "Because I'm trying to be a World Famous Juggler, but I'm not very good at it yet." And he threw the dish and the spoon high in the air, but then—

Tinkle! Tinkle! Crash!

The noise made Lilly jump. She jumped so high, she jumped up through a window and into a house.

"Ow! Ow! Ow!" moaned the dish.

"Ow! Ow! Ow!" groaned the spoon.

"Meeow!"

Lilly looked, and saw a cat sitting on a sofa.

"Hello," said the cat. "What's your name?"

"Lilly," said Lilly.

"Meeow!" the cat mewed again. "My name's Milly. Milly and Lilly! We'd better be friends."

"All right," said Lilly. "But I've come to town because I want to be a World Famous Cow."

"Well how about that?" said Milly. "I'm trying to be a World Famous Musician." She picked up a fiddle and began to play.

Screech! Screech! Screech!

The screeching was so loud that Lilly jumped straight back out the window.

Billy was waiting down below. "That's surprising," he said. "I didn't know cows could jump."

"*I* can," said Lilly.

"How high can you jump?" Billy asked. "As high as I can throw my dish and my spoon?"

Lilly was feeling proud of herself. She looked up at the stars in the dark night sky.

"As high as the moon," she said.

"Nobody can jump as high as that," said Billy.

"I can," said Lilly. "Just watch!"

But when Lilly tried to jump as high as the moon, she ended up on a rooftop instead.

Milly was sitting on a chimney stack. "Meeow!" she mewed in surprise. "What are you doing here?"

"I was trying to jump as high as the moon," Lilly said sadly. "But I couldn't jump high enough."

"Let me play you a jumping tune," said Milly, and she began to play her fiddle.

Screech! Screech! Scratchitty!
Scratchitty scratchitty screech!

"Moo!" said Lilly. "Moo!" And before she knew it she was jumping up and up and up . . . right over the moon.

Down in the street, men and women and children stared and stared and stared.

"**LOOK!**" they said to one another. "Look! A cow jumping over the moon! Whoever heard of a cow that could jump so high!"

The little dog Billy laughed and laughed. He was laughing so much he didn't see the dish and the spoon pick themselves up and dust themselves down.

"All I want is a quiet life," the dish grumbled.

"Me, too," said the spoon.

They looked at each other, shook hands . . . and ran away.

Nobody noticed them going. They were all way too busy cheering for the cow who had jumped right over the moon.

"She'll be a World Famous Cow now," said Billy.

"She most certainly will," said Milly. "You know what, Billy? I think I might try jumping instead of music."

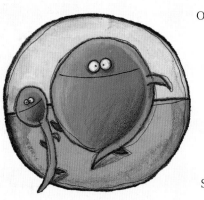

"And I was thinking of jumping instead of juggling," said Billy.

"Let's practice together!" said Milly.

"**Hooray!**" said Billy.

Little Miss Muffet

Little Miss Muffet sat on a tuffet
Eating her curds and whey.
Along came a spider,
Who sat down beside her,
And frightened Miss Muffet away!

Speeder Spider was fed up. No one *ever* wanted to play with him. Every time anyone saw him they shouted, "UGH! It's a **great big horrible hairy spider!**" and ran away.

He found Little Boy Blue asleep under the haystack. When Speeder tickled his nose to wake him up, Little Boy Blue said, "OOOF! Go away!"

He heard Little Bo Peep calling for her sheep in the orchard where he lived.

"Sheep, sheep!" she called. "Where are you?"

"**Coooeee!**" said Speeder hopefully.

"Coooeee!"

But Little Bo Peep ran off, calling, "Sheep! Wait for me!"

When Speeder saw Jack and Jill he didn't bother to follow them. "They've got each other to play with," he said sadly.

Not long after, Speeder saw a little girl walking toward the orchard carrying a blue china bowl. A bigger girl walked behind her carrying a three-legged stool.

Speeder scurried along a branch of the cherry tree to get a better look.

"Here you go, Molly Muffet," said the big girl. She put the stool under Speeder's tree. "You sit here."

"Won't you stay, Tess?" Molly asked. "It's so lovely under the trees."

Tess shuddered. "There might be great big horrible hairy spiders! Now, eat your breakfast."

"But I don't like curds and whey," Molly Muffet said. "It's all **lumpy** and **chunky** and **sticky** and **slimy**."

Tess shook her head. "You *must* eat it, Molly, or Mother will be mad." And she left Molly sitting on her little stool, staring gloomily at her breakfast.

Speeder peered out from under the leaves.

"Little Miss Muffet!" he called. "Little Miss Muffet! Would you like cherries instead?" And he dropped a shiny red cherry onto the grass.

Molly picked it up. "Thank you!" she said. She looked up into the tree to see who was talking to her, but all she could see was leaves. "I *adore* cherries. But Mother will be mad if I don't eat my **lumpy, chunky, sticky, slimy** curds and whey."

"Couldn't you spill it by-mistake-on-purpose?" Speeder suggested.

Molly licked her spoon thoughtfully. "I think Mother would guess. She's very good at guessing things like that."

"What if you had a terrible scare?" Speeder said. "Suppose a **great big horrible hairy spider** came and frightened you?"

"But I'm not frightened of spiders," Molly said. "Tess hates them, but I like them."

Speeder's heart went

pit-a-pit-pat

with excitement. "Could you pretend to be frightened?" he asked.

"Oh, yes," said Molly.

"Then here's the plan!" said Speeder. "I'll come and sit down beside you. You scream and drop your bowl — and everyone will think it's because you're scared!"

Molly stared up into the cherry tree. "Are you a *spider*? Oh, good! I've always wanted a spider as a friend. Come out and say hello!"

"Molly! Molly Muffet!" It was Molly's sister calling from the garden. "Have you eaten your breakfast?"

"*Quick*!" Speeder whispered. "Get ready!"

"I'm almost done," Molly called back.

Just as Tess reached the trees, Speeder sailed down on his silver thread — and sat on the stool beside Molly.

"Oh! Oh! Oh!" shouted Molly. She jumped up, tumbled her bowl into the grass, and ran to her sister.

"OH! OH! OH!" screamed Tess. "It's a great big horrible hairy spider!" She grabbed Molly's hand and rushed her home.

Speeder whizzed up his thread and into his tree to wait. It wasn't long before Molly came running back.

"That was *fun*," she said, her eyes shining. "And look! I've got a plate of bread and strawberry jam! Come and share it."

So Molly and Speeder sat side by side on the tuffet and shared the bread, strawberry jam, and cherries . . . and giggled about what might happen if ever Tess found Speeder in her bowl of curds and whey!

Round and Round the Garden

Round and round the garden,
Like a teddy bear;
One step, two step,
Tickle you under there!

Freddie and Flora were twins. One birthday, Grandma gave them each a teddy bear. Freddie loved Big Ted and took him wherever he went. At night, Big Ted slept on his pillow. Flora loved her Fluffy Ted, but she often left him under the bed, or in the kitchen, or in the bathroom. Fluffy Ted never knew *where* he was going to spend the night . . .

One day Flora took Fluffy Ted out into the garden and forgot to bring him in.

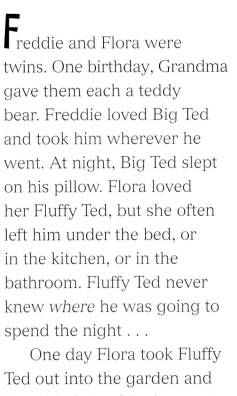

That night, Big Ted did his best to show Flora something was wrong. He wouldn't sit up when Mom put him on a chair to watch the twins having their dinner. He flopped over when Dad was reading a bedtime story. He even slithered off Freddie's pillow and onto the floor, but it was no use. Dad put him back and no one noticed that Fluffy Ted was missing.

"I'll have to go and find him when the twins are asleep." Big Ted decided, and tried not to feel scared.

Big Ted waited until the house was quiet, then slid out of bed. His heart was beating fast as he tiptoed onto the landing. Every noise made him jump.

"The quicker I go, the sooner I'll be safely back in bed," he told himself as he crept down the stairs. He was hurrying toward the back door when *crash!*

Spotty Cat came bouncing through the cat flap.

"Meeow!" said Spotty. "What are *you* doing here?"

"I'm going to fetch Fluffy Ted," said Big Ted as bravely as he could. "Flora left him in the garden. Um . . . is it *very* dark out there?"

"Black as can be!" Spotty said. "Should I hold the cat flap open for you?"

"Oh yes, please," Big Ted said as he wriggled his way out.

"Don't get any fatter while you're outside or you'll get stuck on the way back in!" Spotty said. "See you later!" She let the flap drop down behind Big Ted with a

snap!

Big Ted stood outside the back door and stared into the darkness. He could hear strange little squeaks and creaks.

Eeeeeek!!! Creak!!!

He could hear rustlings and rattlings.

Rustle, rustle . . . Rattle, rattle . . .

He could hear tappings and patterings.

Tap, tap . . . Pitter-patter, pitter-patter . . .

Big Ted swallowed hard and stepped out onto the grass.

"Fluffy Ted!" he whispered in a wobbly voice. "Fluffy Ted! Where are you? I've come to take you home!"

Hoooot! Hooooooot!

An owl flip-flapped over the garden.

"Oh, dear," Big Ted said to himself. "I wish I were back in my warm, cozy bed, all cuddled up beside Freddie! I'll call once more, and if there's still no answer I'll go inside."

Big Ted crept farther into the garden and took a deep breath.

"FLUFFY TED!" he called. "ARE YOU THERE?"

Pit-pat, pit-pat. Pit-pat, pit-pat . . .

What was that behind him? Big Ted froze.

He slowly turned around, and—

JUMPED!

Something soft and tickly was under his nose. **Achoo!** He couldn't help sneezing —

"BIG TED!" cried Fluffy Ted. "It's *me*!"

"Oh, Fluffy Ted!" gasped Big Ted. "I thought you'd be scared out here all by yourself! And instead *you* scared *me*!"

"But I *was* scared, Big Ted," said Fluffy Ted. "I've been **round and round the garden**. It was so dark, I couldn't find the door. Then I heard Spotty talking to you and I thought, *Thank goodness for Big Ted!* I came one step, two steps, and there I was — tickling your nose! But I didn't mean to scare you!"

Fluffy Ted gave Big Ted a great big bear hug. "Am I glad to see you!"

"Come on," said Big Ted happily, "let's go home."

So Big Ted and Fluffy Ted scrambled back through the cat flap and climbed up the stairs to the twins' bedroom. When Flora woke up in the morning she was surprised to see Big Ted and Fluffy Ted cuddled up together on Freddie's pillow.

"Hey!" she said. "That's my bear!" She gave Fluffy Ted a loving squeeze and tucked him under her blankets.

Old King Cole

Old King Cole
Was a merry old soul,
And a merry old soul was he;
He called for his pipe,
And he called for his bowl,
And he called for his fiddlers three.

Old King Cole was angry. He'd lost his pipe and couldn't find it anywhere. He asked the queen, but she said she hadn't seen it.

"Smoking is bad for you," she said.

Old King Cole asked the prime minister, but he didn't know where the pipe was, either. Nor did the three little princes.

"Oh, *rhubarb!*" said Old King Cole. "It's so soothing to blow a smoke ring or two."

As the days went by, Old King Cole gave up smiling. He never

laughed. When the three fiddlers came to play, he sat down and groaned.

"What's the matter with Grandpa?" asked Prince Tom.

"He's lost his pipe," said Prince Jim.

"Well," said Prince Tom, "I think we should find him a new one. Where do you buy pipes?"

"I don't know," said Prince Danny. "Let's ask the prime minister."

"He's too busy to talk to us," said Prince Jim. "Let's ask the boy who cleans the boots."

The boot boy smiled when the princes asked him about pipes.

"My Great Uncle Angus loves pipes," he said. "He's got lots. Should I ask him to come to the palace?"

"Oh yes, please!" said Prince Danny.

"It'll be a wonderful surprise for Grandpa!" said Prince Tom.

"Could you ask him to come this evening?" asked Prince Jim.

"OK," said the boot boy and hurried away.

The afternoon went way too slowly for the three princes. Old King Cole sat and grumbled. When the queen offered him a cup of tea he told her to go away. The queen burst into tears and ran out of the room.

"Don't cry, Grandma," said Prince Tom.

"We're going to surprise Grandpa tonight!" said Prince Jim.

Prince Danny whispered, "We're getting him lots of new pipes!"

"But smoking is *bad* for him!" The queen sobbed. "That's why I threw his pipe away! I never thought it would make him so grumpy!"

"He'll be all right tonight," Prince Tom said. "Just wait and see!"

The queen wiped her eyes. "Maybe it *is* a good idea to let him have his pipe back," she said. "I can't bear him being so miserable."

The evening came at last. The fiddlers came marching in to play their fiddles, and the three princes began to look hopefully at the door.

"Tonight," said the first fiddler, "we have a special tune for your majesty!"

EEeeeeeeeeeeeeeEEEEEEEeeeeeeeeeeEEEEEEEeeeeeeeeeEEEEEEeee!!!

The wailing noise made even Old King Cole sit up. The queen's eyes opened wide and the princes hid behind the throne.

EEeeeeeeeeeeeeeEEEEEEEeeeeeeeeee EEEEEEEEeeeeeeeeeEEEEEEeee!!!

The door opened and in strode the boot boy's great uncle Angus, playing the bagpipes.

"I'm here with the pipes, your majesty," said Great Uncle Angus, and he began to play a rollicking tune.

The fiddlers joined in. The princes snapped their fingers and Old King Cole leaped up from his throne.

"Two plums and a fig, let's dance a jig!"

he shouted, seizing the queen and whirling her round and round.

Faster went the pipes. Faster went the fiddles. Faster went Old King Cole . . . until at last the music stopped.

"Phew!" said Old King Cole as he wiped his forehead. "That was *great*! Piper! I shall be calling for you every evening!"

Great Uncle Angus bowed.

"And . . . would you teach me how to play?"

Great Uncle Angus bowed again and Old King Cole picked up the bagpipes. AAAAAAAAAaaaaaaaAAAAAAAaa aaaaaaAAAAAAAAaaaaaaooooooo!!! Yowliewowliewooooooooooooooo!!!

Everyone put their hands over their ears — but Old King Cole was the merriest man in the kingdom.

Jack and Jill

Jack and Jill went up the hill,
To fetch a pail of water;
Jack fell down and broke his crown,
And Jill came tumbling after.

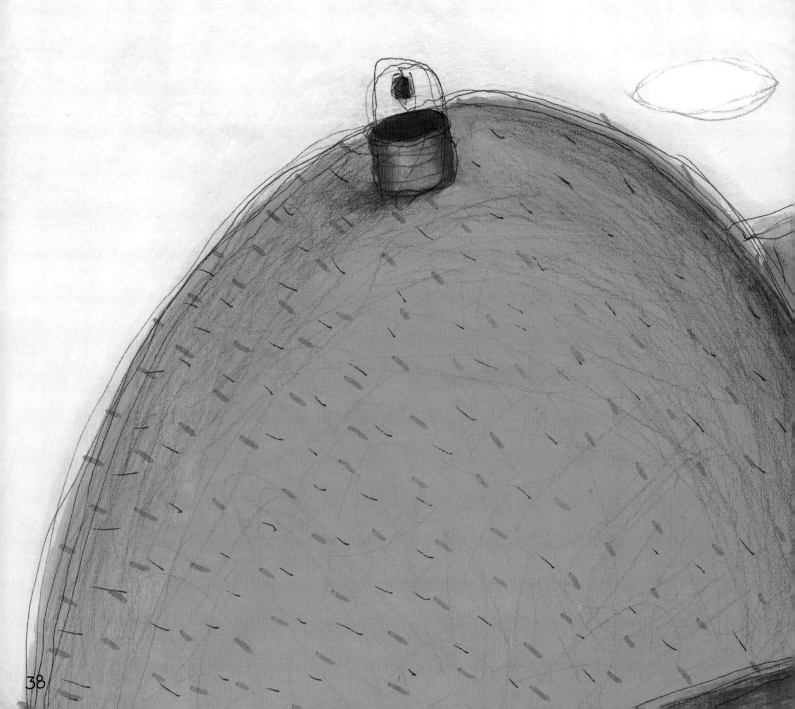

Everyone said Jack was a good boy. He helped his mama fetch the water from the well at the top of the hill and he helped her hang the laundry. He kept his toys tidy and was always neat and clean.

No one said Jill was a good girl. She was messy and left her toys all over the floor. When she helped her mama she spilled the water and she trailed the just-washed laundry in the mud.

All the same, her mama and Jack loved her and she loved them back.

One fine Wednesday, Great Grandma Brown came over for breakfast. Jack and Jill were playing hide-and-seek and Great Grandma didn't see Jill hiding under the table.

"That boy Jack is a *good* boy," Great Grandma told Mama. "He deserves a treat. The fair is coming to town on Saturday, so I'll take him. What's more, he shall have his very own silver dollar to spend."

"That's kind," Mama said. "But what about our Jill? She doesn't mean to be naughty."

"**HUMPH!**" said Great Grandma. "The day I see your Jill doing something right is the day I dance on my **feathery** hat. But fair's fair. If that day comes by Saturday, I'll take her, too. And I'll give her a silver dollar. But you're not to tell Jill, mind!"

Mama sighed. She didn't think Jill would ever do anything right by Saturday . . . but she didn't know Jill was listening to every word.

When Great Grandma Brown had gone, Jill sat very still. She wanted to go to the fair. She wanted a silver dollar. But, most of all, she really, *really* wanted to see Great Grandma Brown dance on her **feathery** hat.

That night, Jill tidied up *all* the toys. Her mama couldn't believe her eyes.

On Thursday, Jill set the table without being asked. Her mama was so shocked she had to sit down.

On Friday, Jill got up early and tiptoed downstairs. Jack heard her and followed her into the kitchen.

"What are you doing?" he asked.

"I'm going to fetch the water for Mama," Jill said. "I'm being good."

"Why?" Jack asked.

Jill put her finger to her lips. "Shhh! It's a secret! I'll tell you at the top of the hill!"

Jack fetched the pail and they hurried up the hill together. When they got to the top, Jack put the bucket down.

"Tell me the secret!" he said.

"If Great Grandma sees me doing something good," Jill told him, "she'll dance on her **feathery** hat! So I'll keep

on doing good things until she sees me!"

Jack's eyes sparkled. "Aha!" he shouted, and jumped in the air — and fell over the bucket. Down the hill he rolled.

Bumpetty bumpetty bump!

Jill tried to stop him, but she fell, too—
Bumpetty bumpetty bump!

"**OUCH!**" Jack wailed. "My head!"

"Poor Jack," Jill said. "Let me rub it better." And so she did — just as Great Grandma came stomping around the corner.

"What's going on here?" she asked.

"Jill's making me better," Jack said. "I fell over."

Great Grandma Brown stared at Jill. Then she took off her great big **feathery** hat and danced up and down on it until it was flat as a pancake

"Jack and Jill," she said, "you'd better be ready first thing tomorrow. I'm taking you both to the fair."

The next day, when Jack and Jill came back from the fair, Jack was laughing . . . and covered in mud.

Jill was laughing . . . and neat as a pin.

Mary, Mary, Quite Contrary

Mary, Mary, quite contrary,
How does your garden grow?
With silver bells and cockleshells,
And pretty maids all in a row.

Mary Minnipeg was a mermaid. She lived at the bottom of the sea with her mom and her dad and a crab named James. In the cave next door lived Mary's aunt and her six girl cousins. Every girl cousin had beautiful long hair, big round eyes, and a lovely smile. Mary had short hair, a turned-up nose, and a **fearsome** frown. Mary thought the six girl cousins were **silly**. They thought she was **grumpy**.

Mary's mom liked lying on a rock and singing. Her dad liked diving through the waves and laughing. Mary and James didn't like singing OR laughing. They liked sitting in their cave playing Snap.

When Mary won she said, "Good!"

When James won he clicked his claws.

Neither of them ever smiled.

"Mary," her mom said one day, "why don't you come and sing with me?"

"No, thank you," Mary said.

"Come and dive through the waves with me," said her dad. "It'll be fun!"

"No, thank you," said Mary. "I don't want fun."

"Come and play dress up," said her six girl cousins.

"No, thank you," said Mary. "I want to play Snap."

And Mary and James went on playing Snap, until one morning Mary woke up and found the cards scattered all over the floor. James was gone.

Her mom said she was very sorry about James, but now Mary could come and lie

on a rock and sing.

Mary said she didn't want to.

Her dad said he was very sorry, too, but now Mary could try diving through the waves.

Mary said she didn't want to.

Her mom and dad both sighed. "She's so **contrary**," said her mom as they swam away.

Mary went to the cave next door.

"Does anyone want to play Snap?" she asked, frowning fiercely.

"No, no, no!" sang the six cousins. "But you can play with us! Today we're dressing up as princesses — look what we have in our treasure chest!"

Mary looked. She saw heaps and heaps of pebbles and pearls and shells and shiny glass, and all kinds of other bits and pieces tumbled together.

"See?" said her oldest cousin. "I'm sure you could be a princess if you dressed up!"

"Humph!" said Mary. "I don't want to be a princess. I'm going to be a gardener instead. I shall make a garden for my best friend James so he'll come back and play Snap with me." Mary scooped up two heaping handfuls from the treasure chest and hurried away.

The six girl cousins waved good-bye and went on dressing up in necklaces and bracelets and crowns.

After a while the littlest one said, "What does a garden look like?"

Her older sisters had no idea, so the littlest one said, "Can we go and see Mary's garden?"

And the other five sang, "Oh, yes, yes, yes!"

They tiptoed on their tails to the door of their cave and peeked out.

49

50

"**Ooooooooh!**" they all said together. "It's beautiful!"

And it was.

There were rows and rows of cockleshells and silver bells, and little bits of glittering green glass. There were swirly patterns of polished pebbles, and floaty seaweed that looked like an enchanted forest. Right in the middle were shimmery pearls carefully arranged to spell out:

PLEASE COME HOME, JAMES.

The six pretty mermaids stood in a row and stared.

"You are *so* smart, Mary," said the oldest. "Will you show *us* how to make a garden?"

Mary looked at them thoughtfully. "I might," she said, "if you play Snap with me later."

The cousins all nodded. "YES!" they said.

And for the very first time in her life, Mary Minnipeg smiled. . . .

And James, who'd been hiding behind a rock because he was so very, very tired of playing Snap, clicked his claws happily and came out to play in his garden.

Hickory, Dickory, Dock

Hickory, dickory, dock,
The mouse ran up the clock.
The clock struck one,
The mouse ran down,
Hickory, dickory, dock.

Squeak squeak squeak!

Martha Ninepenny liked mice. She liked them a lot.

Her mom hated them. She said they were dirty. Her dad did, too. He said mice were messy.

That's why Martha never told anyone there was a little gray mouse living under the great big grandfather clock in the hall.

Martha was happy she had a mouse as a friend. Her mom never had time to play with her because she was too busy washing things. Her dad didn't have time to play with her because he was too busy working. Rosie, the girl next door, looked nice, but she'd only just moved in and Martha was much too shy to speak to her. As a matter of fact, Martha Ninepenny would have been very bored indeed if it hadn't been for George.

Martha knew the little gray mouse's name was George because he had told her so. She also knew he loved cake, but he didn't ever get to eat more than a crumb because he had a mouse mother, two aunts, and five baby sisters who all liked cake, too.

"Do they live under the clock with you?" Martha asked. "I've never seen them."

George turned very pink. "Actually, I don't *live* there," he explained. "I *hide* there when my mother tells me to clean our nest."

Martha Ninepenny nodded. "My mom's always telling me to clean my room," she said.

One day, Martha received an invitation to Rosie's party. She was terribly excited. She lay on her tummy by the grandfather clock and whispered to George.

"I'm going to Rosie's party this afternoon! I've wanted to be friends with Rosie ever since she moved next door, but I've been too shy to talk to her!"

"Martha Ninepenny! Whatever are you doing?" It was her mom. "Have you cleaned your room yet?"

55

Martha jumped up. "Is it time to go?"

"No," Mom said. "Not until you've taken a bath and washed your hair."

Martha rushed upstairs. She ran into her room and flung her clothes on the floor. Then she dashed into the bathroom and jumped into the bath. When she finished, she skipped into her bedroom — and found her mom waiting for her.

"MARTHA NINEPENNY!"

she said. "*Look* at this mess! There'll be *no* party for you until you've cleaned your room. You've got until the clock strikes one."

Martha gave a little gasp. "How long is that?" she asked.

"Ten minutes exactly," Mom said and shut the door behind her.

Martha began to cry.

"Squeak! Squeak!"

George darted out from under a cupboard. "Don't cry," he said. "I'll help you!"

"But you're too small," Martha wailed. "I'll never get my entire room tidied up in ten minutes!"

George twirled his whiskers. "I've got an idea," he said. "Didn't your mom say you had to clean up before the clock struck one?"

Martha nodded.

"Then we'll stop the clock!" said George. "You get busy. I'll take care of the clock!"

Martha smiled. "Thank you," she whispered.

Martha folded her clothes and put them away. She put her toys into their box. Then she looked around. Her room had never ever been so tidy.

"MOM!" she called,

"MOM!"

Her mother came up the stairs. "Goodness me," she said. "That's wonderful!" Then she looked at her watch. "But I did say it had to be clean *before* one o'clock —"

Boing!

Downstairs the clock struck one. Martha's mom shook her head. "My watch must be fast," she said. "Good job, Martha!"

As she ran next door to Rosie's party, Martha called out,

"THANK YOU, GEORGE!"

And then she added, "I'll bring back a *big* slice of cake, just for you!"

Squeak! Squeak! Squeak!

pat-a-Cake

Pat-a-cake, pat-a-cake, baker's man,
Bake me a cake as fast as you can.
Pat it and prick it and mark it with a *B*,
Put it in the oven for Baby and me.

Mr. and Mrs. Button's house was so tall and narrow that some of their things were always bursting out of it. Sometimes it was a saucepan that came whizzing through a window.

Whizzzzzzzzzzzzz!!!

Sometimes it was a pair of boots.

Wheeeeeeeeeee!!!

Sometimes it was the cat.

Meerrrrrrrow!!!

And today it was the baby.

The mailman caught the baby and took it back at once.

Bobby Button opened the door. He was the oldest boy.

"Yours, I believe?" said the mailman, and he handed him the baby.

"Ooops," said Bobby. "Mom was wondering where she'd gone."

The mailman peered at the baby. "Good-looking baby," he said. "How old?"

"She's one today," Bobby said.

"Well how do you like that!" The mailman beamed. "Happy Birthday—er—what's your name?"

"She doesn't talk yet," Bobby said. "She goes, 'Goo goo goo!'"

"Goo goo goo!" said the baby.

"But she does have a name?" the mailman asked.

Bobby turned red. "Mom and Dad can't make up their minds, so we just call her Baby," he said.

"No name? Dear me!" The mailman patted the baby's head. "Hope you'll be having a nice big birthday cake!"

"**Goo!**" said the baby enthusiastically. "**Goo goo goo!**"

Bobby turned even redder. "Mom made three cakes today, and she burned them all, as usual."

The mailman looked shocked. "Well I never!" he said, and he fished in his pocket. "No name and no cake. We can't have that! Here's a shiny silver dollar. You run along to the baker right now and buy this young lady a cake!"

"**Oohh!**" said Bobby. "Thank you!" He swung the baby up onto his shoulders. "Come on, Baby! We're off to the baker's to buy you a cake!"

The bakery was empty when Bobby arrived.

"Hello," said the baker's man, "may I help you?"

"We'd like a cake, please," said Bobby. "A cake for Baby."

"Be with you in a minute," said the man, and he went off to the back of the shop.

A little girl came running in the door. She looked at the baby sitting on Bobby's shoulders and smiled.

"What's your name?" she asked.

The baby looked at her and smiled back. "**Cakie!**" she said.

The little girl clapped her hands. "Katie? But that's my name! I'm Katie, too! Hello, Katie!"

Bobby's eyes were very wide. "**Wow**," he said. "Baby spoke! That's her first word ever!"

63

Just then the baker's man came back with a big box. "Here's your cake," he said to Bobby. "And I've put a **B** on it for Baby!"

"Thank you," said Bobby, and he turned to go.

The little girl called, "Good-bye, Katie!" and the baby waved.

Bobby rushed through his front door.

"Mom!" he shouted. "Mom! Baby said her first word! And look what we've got!" He opened the box. Inside was a pink cake with one pink candle and a big letter **B** on top.

"**B** for Baby!" said Bobby. "Look, Baby!"

"Waaaaaaaaa!" The baby suddenly began to scream. "Cakie!"

"Shhhh, Baby," said Mrs. Button, and she cut a slice of cake. "There! Happy Birthday, Baby!"

"Waaaaaaaaa!" yelled the baby, and threw her spoon on the floor. "Cakie! Cakie! CAKIE!"

All the Buttons stared at the baby.

"What's the matter with her?" asked Mr. Button.

Bobby scratched his ear. "Actually," he said, "I think Baby's given *herself* a name." He looked at his sister, who was still yelling.

"Hey! Are you Katie?"

The baby stopped at once and beamed.

"Katie!" she said clearly. "Katie cake!"

"But what about the **B** for Baby?" asked Mr. Button. "It's already on the cake!"

"**B** for Button!" said Bobby. He leaned over and drew a **K** beside the **B**.

"Happy Birthday, Katie Button!"

And Katie Button gave her brother a big sticky kiss.

Humpty Dumpty

Humpty Dumpty sat on a wall,
Humpty Dumpty had a great fall;
All the king's horses and all the king's men
Couldn't put Humpty together again.

Charlie Apricot was the cook's new helper in the kitchen at the royal palace. He was very excited. Cook had told him he could take breakfast to the little princess. He'd never met a princess before. Come to think of it, he'd never met a cook before.

Cook was quite ordinary, except when she got angry. When she was fed up, she threw plates all around the kitchen.

Crash! Crash! Crash!

Luckily, she only threw plates at walls — not at people — so Charlie didn't mind.

Soon, he became very good at mending the broken plates with the pot of glue Cook gave him.

Charlie couldn't wait to meet the princess, but when he finally did he was very disappointed. She was called Princess Daisy, but she looked exactly like any other little girl — apart from the crown. What's more, before Charlie had even said "Hello," Daisy was ordering him to play dolls with her, and he couldn't get away. He hoped and hoped Cook would call for him, but she didn't.

The next day, when Cook asked Charlie to take Princess Daisy her breakfast, he asked if he had to.

"Yes," Cook said firmly.

Charlie sighed. "But I don't like playing with dolls."

"Play something else, then," Cook told him.

So when Princess Daisy wanted to play with dolls, Charlie showed her how to play Snakes and Ladders. And hide-and-seek. And soccer. By the end of the week he was good friends with the princess . . . but he was worried because it was her birthday on Saturday and he didn't have a present for her. He asked Cook what he should do, but she said she was *much* too hot and bothered about baking for Princess Daisy's birthday party to think of anything else. She gave Charlie a pile of broken plates and the queen's best teapot to mend. Charlie continued to worry.

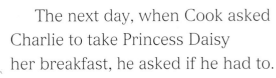

Princess Daisy's birthday arrived. The king and the queen gave her a great big china egg doll and she loved it. She named it Humpty Dumpty and carried it with her all morning.

When it was time for her birthday parade, Princess Daisy insisted that Humpty Dumpty go with her to watch. Charlie was sitting on the palace wall and Princess Daisy climbed up beside him.

"Don't sit up there, dear," said the queen. "Sit down here on your throne!"

But Princess Daisy stuck out her lip. "But I *want* to sit on the wall with Charlie Apricot and Humpty Dumpty!" she said.

The queen sighed and said, "Very well, dear. It *is* your birthday."

All the king's horses and all the king's men marched up and down and blew their trumpets. And then — **boom!** They fired a huge gun in honor of Princess Daisy's birthday. The princess jumped and Charlie jumped. The wall shook, and — **crash!**

Humpty Dumpty fell off and broke into pieces.

Princess Daisy cried and cried. All the king's horses and all the king's men came running to her side, but they couldn't help. And neither could the king or the queen.

Nobody could stop Daisy from crying . . . until Charlie had a *brilliant* idea! He dashed off to the palace and soon came running back with his pot of glue.

He mended Humpty Dumpty even better than he'd mended the queen's teapot. Daisy said that was the best birthday present she could ever have. She gave Charlie a *huge* hug.

When the king, the queen, all the king's horses and all the king's men, and Princess Daisy sat down to Cook's special birthday banquet,

Princess Daisy asked Charlie to
sit next to her.
  "Dear Charlie Apricot," she said,

offering him the very first slice of cake. "If I promise not to make you play with dolls, will you be the Royal Best Friend?"

Charlie said, "Yes, please!"

Baa, Baa, Black Sheep

Baa, baa, black sheep,
Have you any wool?
Yes sir, yes sir,
Three bags full.
One for the master,
One for the dame,
And one for the little boy
Who lives down the lane.

Mickey MacMuffler lived in a very small cottage at the end of Muddle Lane. His daddy, Master MacMuffler, was a shepherd who kept his flock on the high green hills. Every summer he went away to find them and catch them and shear off their wool, but Mickey didn't mind. His grandma, Dame MacMuffler, looked after him when his dad was gone. She was a wonderful teller of stories. She was also a champion knitter. Every year she won first prize at the county fair for her scarves and her mittens and her hats and her blankets.

In fact, Dame MacMuffler was so busy knitting that she never had time to cook. She never had time to clean. She never dug the garden or picked up sticks for the fire. She never painted the walls or hammered in a nail. She sat in her chair all day and every day, telling Mickey stories and **knit-knit-knitting.**

Luckily, Mickey could cook. And clean. And he was good at finding sticks for the fire and growing potatoes, so they were very happy together until one day when the northeast wind

blew

and

blew

and

BLEW.

By the end of the morning the very small cottage had begun to creak.

Wheeeeeeeeeeeeeeeeeeeee! blew the wind.

By lunchtime the wind was groaning.

Whoooooooooooooooooooooo! it blew.

Just before dinner, the roof blew off the cottage.

Wheeeeeeooooooooeeeee eeeooooooeeeeeeee! blew the wind.

Mickey stood staring with his mouth wide open. Dame MacMuffler sat calmly in her chair, **knit-knit-knitting**.

"Mickey dear," she said. "Run up into the hills and fetch your daddy home from shearing, there's a good boy. We can't live in a house with no roof. If it rains, my knitting needles will get rusty and I'll never make another pair of mittens or win another prize."

So Mickey ran down the lane and up into the hills, the wind **whirling round and round and round** him.

He found a hill full of white sheep with thick white woolly fleeces, but he didn't find his daddy.

He found a hill full of spotted sheep with long spotted fleeces, but his daddy wasn't there, either.

He found a hill full of black sheep with neat clipped coats and a heap of sacks stuffed with thick black wool — but he still couldn't find his daddy.

The sun sank low into the clouds and the sky grew dark. Mickey sat down among the sacks of black wool and blew his nose hard. He was trying not to cry.

"Baa!"

said a voice. "*Baa!* You're the master's son, aren't you? What's the matter with you?"

Mickey rubbed his eyes. A big black sheep was standing right beside him. "I can't find my daddy!" said Mickey. "The roof's blown off our house and Grandma says that if it rains her knitting needles will rust and she'll

never be able to win another prize! Oh, please can you help?"

"*Baa*," said the sheep as she looked up into the sky. "It's a fine night tonight," she said. "And my toe bones tell me it'll be a fine day tomorrow. That should be time enough."

"Time enough for what?" asked Mickey.

"Time enough for Dame MacMuffler to save the day!" said the sheep. "Choose three bags of wool and take them home: one for you, one for the master, and one for the dame. There's just enough time for a champion knitter like your Grandma to knit you a brand-new roof."

"Thank you very much," said Mickey and chose the three biggest bags.

"Now," said the sheep, "you run along home and I'll find the master for you."

"Thank you!" Mickey said again. He hugged the sheep and picked up the bags of wool. Then he ran and ran until he was home.

"Grandma!" he said as he burst through the door. "I have enough wool here for you to knit us a new roof!"

"Oh, Mickey!" said Dame MacMuffler. "What a clever boy you are!"

All night long she knitted.

Knit-knit-knit-knit-knit-knit-knit . . .

And all the next day . . .

By evening the cottage had a brand-new black woolly roof. It kept the cottage so warm, Mickey had to open all the windows. As he opened the very last window he looked out — and there was his daddy walking home with a black sheep close beside him . . . just as the rain began.

Georgie Porgie

Georgie Porgie, pudding and pie,
Kissed the girls and made them cry;
When the boys came out to play,
Georgie Porgie ran away.

Georgie Porgie was a
naughty little piglet. He
crept into the larder and
ate a big bread pudding.

Then he ate an
enormous apple pie.

Mother Pig was very
angry indeed when
she found him licking the
pie dish.

"You're a bad little
pig!" she told him. "Go and
play outside!"

Lucy Lamb and Clara Calf were skipping in the yard with Georgie Porgie's six little sisters.

"I'll twirl the rope," Georgie said, but he twirled it too fast.

"Go away, Georgie Porgie," said Clara. "You're spoiling our game!"

"Skipping's silly," Georgie said. "Let's play Kiss Chase!" And he rushed toward his littlest sister, Peggy, shouting, "**Kiss! Kiss! Kiss!**"

Peggy squealed loudly and ran away as fast as she could go. Georgie ran after her and grabbed her by her little curly tail.

"Caught you!" he shouted and gave her a kiss. Peggy began to cry and Georgie ran toward Lucy.

"Your turn!" he called, but when he kissed Lucy she began to cry as well.

"Go *away*, Georgie!" Clara said angrily. "You're spoiling *everything*!"

"Can't catch me!" yelled Georgie as he scrambled up to the top of the haystack.

"Ha ha ha, hee hee hee — I'm on a haystack and you can't catch me!"

Clara, Lucy, and his six little piglet sisters stared up at him.

"You're mean, Georgie Porgie," said Lucy. "I'm going to tell my big brother, Larry!"

"And *I'm* going to tell my big brother, Carlo!" said Clara.

"Hey, diddle, dumpling, see if you dare! I'm on a haystack and I don't care!" sang naughty Georgie Porgie as he danced up and down and threw hay at them.

"**Baa!**" bleated Lucy as she trotted off to find Larry.

"**Mooo!**" mooed Clara as she hurried off to find Carlo.

Peggy and her five sisters scurried away home.

Georgie Porgie danced on top of the haystack . . . until he saw Larry and Carlo stamping into the yard, looking very angry.

"**Ooops!**" said Georgie and buried himself in hay.

"Come down, Georgie Porgie!" bleated Larry.

"Come and play with us, Georgie Porgie!" bellowed Carlo.

Georgie Porgie said nothing at all. He stayed as still as could be on the top of the haystack. Larry and Carlo looked at each other.

"Shall we play soccer here in the yard?" asked Larry and winked.

Carlo winked back. "Good idea," he said.

Larry and Carlo played a *long* game of soccer. Georgie Porgie waited for them to go away . . . but they didn't. When they'd finished playing soccer they played long jump. And then they played high jump. And then they played soccer again.

Georgie Porgie began to feel very hungry.

At last, Lucy came to call Larry home for his dinner. Clara came with Lucy and she told Carlo his dinner was ready, too. Nobody came to tell Georgie Porgie that his dinner was ready. As soon as Carlo and Larry left he slid down the haystack and ran home.

"Mother! Mother! Mother!" he squealed as he dashed through the door. "I'm *starving*!"

"But Peggy told me you were playing with the boys," said Mother Pig. "She said you weren't hungry."

"But I am!" wailed Georgie.

"Oh dearie me," Mother Pig said. "We've eaten nearly *all* the rhubarb ice cream!" She looked at the six little girl piglets. "Shall we let Georgie have the last helping?"

"**NO!**" said Peggy. Then she giggled. "Well — not unless he lets us chase *him* around the yard tomorrow!"

Twinkle, Twinkle, Little Star

Twinkle, twinkle, little star,
How I wonder what you are!
Up above the world so high,
Like a diamond in the sky.

The sun was slowly sinking behind the purple western hills, and behind the evening clouds the stars were getting ready to slip into the dark blue sky.

"Tonight," said a large and glittering star, "my brothers and I will shine over the ships at sea. The sailors will look out for us, and steer their ships safely home."

"Tonight," said a star who was as bright as a new pin, "my family and I will light up the soft dark velvet of the southern skies. Men and women will be dazzled, and many will fall in love."

"Tonight," said a gleaming star with a thousand silver sisters, "we will spangle the heavens with our beauty. Travelers will stop and wonder at us, and then go on their way refreshed by our presence."

A little star heard what the others were saying, and he snuggled close beside his mother.

"How important they are," he said. "I could never be as grand as they are."

"They think far too much of themselves," said his mother, sniffing. "Every star is there to sparkle for someone. They just want to make a fuss about it and show off."

"I'd like to sparkle for the children,"

said the little star, sighing, "but by the time we come out, they're tucked into bed. I try to see in through their windows, but

they're listening to their mommies and daddies reading them a story, and they don't see me. Or else they're already fast asleep. I try to twinkle in their dreams, but it's just not the same. I do wish I could shine a little earlier . . . just as the sun goes down."

"What's that? What's that? A little star who's not happy?" It was the moon, and she was looking most surprised.

The little star's mother blushed. "I'm so sorry, my lady," she said. "He's a young star still, and he doesn't know what he's saying."

"Yes I do!" said the little star eagerly. "I do, I do! I want to watch over **Little Miss Muffet** as her mother calls her to come inside! I want to be shining high in the sky when **Jack and Jill** peek out of their window just one last time before they go to sleep! And . . . ," the little star gave a huge sigh, "and then they'd all know I'd be there if they woke up from a bad dream, and they'd smile before snuggling deep down into their pillows."

The moon looked thoughtful. "I suppose it could be allowed," she said. "I'm very fond of children myself . . . But wouldn't you be lonely up in the sky all on your own?"

"Oh, no, not at all!" exclaimed the little star. "I'd be so happy . . . and besides, by the time the children were sleeping, all my brothers and sisters and cousins would be sparkling all around me!"

The moon smiled at the eager little star. "Very well, then," she said. "So be it! Come with me and we'll go up into the sky together!"

The little star blew his mother a kiss, and then floated up and up into the velvet evening sky behind the silver moon. And he

twinkled,
twinkled,
twinkled

as he'd never done before. Far below on Earth the children saw him, and smiled and waved at their very own star.

And if you look up into the evening sky, just as the sun has set, you'll see the little star **twinkling** all on his own . . .

just
for you.

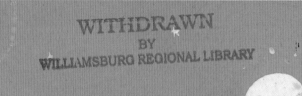